CREATURE CAMPERS

THE SECRET OF SHADOW LAKE

JOE McGEE   BEA TORMO

HAVE YOU HEARD ABOUT EPIC! YET?

We're the largest digital library for kids, used by millions in homes and schools around the world. We love stories so much that we're now creating our own!

With the help of some of the best writers and illustrators in the world, we create the wildest adventures we can think of. Like a mermaid and narwhal who solve mysteries. Or a pet made out of slime.

We hope you have as much fun reading our books as we had making them!

epic! originals

CREATURE CAMPERS

THE SECRET OF SHADOW LAKE

JOE McGEE

ILLUSTRATED BY BEA TORMO

Andrews McMeel
PUBLISHING®

CREATURE CAMPERS
THE SECRET OF SHADOW LAKE

Andrews McMeel Publishing
a division of Andrews McMeel Universal
1130 Walnut Street, Kansas City, Missouri 64106

www.andrewsmcmeel.com

Epic! Creations, Inc.
702 Marshall Street, Suite 280, Redwood City, California 94063

www.getepic.com

20 21 22 23 24 SHD 10 9 8 7 6 5 4 3 2

Paperback ISBN: 978-1-5248-5518-5
Hardback ISBN: 978-1-5248-5546-8

Library of Congress Control Number: 2019941923

Design by Ariana Abud and Wendy Gable

Made by:
Sheridan Books, Inc.
Address and location of manufacturer:
613 E. Industrial Drive
Chelsea, Michigan 48118
2nd Printing—5/22/20

"Hurry up, Norm!" called Ma. "You don't want to be late for your first day of camp."

That was *exactly* what Norm wanted. In fact, he didn't want to go to camp at all.

Norm stared into the bathroom mirror. His belly button stared back at him. He tried to squat down so that he could see his face, but his knees bumped the sink.

He still could only see himself from the shoulders down.

"Stupid growth spurt," he mumbled.

It's not like he asked for this body. One day he could walk without tripping over his own feet, and the next day . . . *WHOOM*! He was taller than Pa. And he wasn't even a teenager yet!

Norm leaned to the left and kicked over the clothes hamper. He leaned to the right and lost his balance, pulling the shower curtain down. He tugged the shower curtain off his head, tripped on the laundry, stumbled over the trash can, and fell back into the bathtub.

"Everything okay up there?" called Ma.

"Just combing my hair!" Norm said with a high-pitched squeak. Even his voice was determined to make his life miserable. He sat in the empty tub and pulled a very big comb across the tops of his enormous, furry feet.

"That's my boy!" said Pa, popping into the bathroom. "Big shoes to fill! Get it? Because you're a Bigfoot!"

Norm groaned.

"What's with the attitude?" said Pa. "When I was your age . . ."

"I know, Pa, I know," said Norm. "I should be super excited that you're sending me to Camp Moonlight. You had to beg Gram and Pop-Pop to go."

Norm pulled the corners of his mouth into a big grin. "See? Super excited."

Pa crossed his arms over his hairy chest. "Oh yeah, I can feel the excitement."

"Maybe it's just not for me," said Norm.

"What are you worried about?"

"That I won't fit in," said Norm. "I barely fit in this bathroom. I'll be taller than all of the other campers. And hairier. And my feet are enormous!"

"You're a Bigfoot," said Pa. "Not a 'smallfoot.' Your size is perfectly normal. Besides, you know what they say at Camp Moonlight. Being different is not unusual . . . it's *FUNusual.*"

Norm rolled his eyes. If there was a prize for dorkiest camp motto, Camp Moonlight would be the winner.

"Just give it a chance," said Pa.

"On one condition," said Norm.

Pa arched an eyebrow.

"Help me up out of this tub? I think I'm stuck."

"Here we are," said Pa. "Camp Moonlight!"

Ma clapped her hands together. "Oh, the memories," she sighed.

"Uh, where's the camp?" asked Norm. "All I see are the same woods we've been trekking through for the last four hours."

"You're looking right at it," said Pa. He winked at Norm.

Ma giggled.

"Riiight." Norm folded his lanky arms across his chest. "Can we go home now?"

"Welcome to Camp Moonlight!" said a gruff voice.

Norm jumped back, almost knocking Ma and Pa over.

"Whoa! Did you hear that?" said Norm. "That tree stump is talking."

"I am *not* a stump," said the gruff voice.

A very small, very grumpy gnome in a patchwork cap emerged from behind the stump. "I am your camp director, Furrow Grumplestick," he said. He lifted up a clipboard bigger than himself and ran his pencil down the list. "You must be . . ."

"Ginormous!" Pa said.

Grumplestick surveyed Norm from head to toe. "Yes, yes you are," he said.

"No, that's my name," said Norm. "Ginormous Strider. But everyone calls me Norm."

Grumplestick scratched his eyebrow with his pencil. "Norm it is."

"Can someone please explain why I don't see a camp?" said Norm. "Where are the cabins? Where is the dining hall? Where are all of the other campers?"

Grumplestick pushed his cap back with his pencil.

"You ask a lot of questions." He chewed on his eraser a moment and then scribbled something on the paper attached to his clipboard.

"What are you writing?" asked Norm. "Is that about me?"

Grumplestick ignored Norm's question while continuing to scribble.

"Ah, here comes another camper now," said Grumplestick.

It took Norm a second to figure out what he was looking at. This skinny creature was taller than Grumplestick, but not by much. It had no fur. No tail. No wings. Its teeth weren't even pointy.

It was a human!

"Oliver Fitzpatrick," said Grumplestick. He checked his name off the list. "Welcome to Camp Moonlight."

"Thanks?" squeaked Oliver, who stood in the middle of a pair of sturdy-looking forest rangers like a pebble between two boulders.

Oliver's gaze was fixed on Norm.

"Don't stare," said Oliver's mom. "It's not polite."

"You're going to be campmates," said Oliver's dad. He grabbed Oliver's shoulder and gave it a playful shake. "I bet you two will be best of friends in no time." When his dad let go, Oliver dizzily stumbled forward.

Norm put out his hand to stop him from falling face-first into his fur. "See?" said Oliver's dad. "Friends already."

"I think we're at the wrong camp," squeaked Oliver.

Grumplestick scrunched his eyebrows together and checked his list again.

"Nope, you're right here on my list. Oliver Fitzpatrick."

Oliver gulped. "But I'm a *human.*"

"Yep, that's what's on my list," said Grumplestick. "Oliver Fitzpatrick. Human."

"Are there . . . *other* humans?" Oliver asked.

Grumplestick scratched his patchwork cap with his pencil before running down the list. "Let's see . . . centaur, pixie, jackalope, blah, blah, mothboy, unicorn, chupacabra, blah, blah, blah, goblin, gremlin, mermaid . . . nope. You're it."

Norm cleared his throat and gave Oliver a big, toothy smile. "If it makes you feel any better, I'm pretty sure I'm the only Bigfoot here."

Oliver gulped. "You're not going to eat me, right?"

Norm quickly pressed his lips together. *Eat him?* Maybe next time he should show less teeth.

MEANWHILE...

What Norm didn't know was that someone was watching them from the tippy top of a towering tree. That someone was none other than the world-famous collector of rare creatures, the curator of curiosities, the connoisseur of cryptozoology . . .

AHEM, CAN YOU GET ON WITH IT, PLEASE?

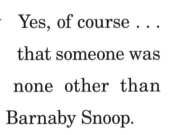

Yes, of course . . . that someone was none other than Barnaby Snoop.

Barnaby sneered. "A Bigfoot will be the perfect contribution to my collection! Nothing will keep me from capturing you for my carnival of creatures. NOTHING!"

Barnaby looked down at the ground, so very far below him.

"Except for getting out of this tree," he said. "It's really quite scary up here."

He twisted the ends of his mustache. "But after that, nothing will get in my way!"

"Alright campers," said Grumplestick, "follow me."

"Where exactly are we going?" Oliver squeaked.

Norm followed the clipboard-clutching gnome. "I don't see any . . . WOW!"

As they passed between two towering pine trees, the forest was suddenly gone.

Well, not completely gone. It was still all around them, on the outskirts of Camp Moonlight. But now there were tents and cabins of different shapes and sizes. In the center of the clearing stood a pole even taller than Norm with a Camp Moonlight flag gently flapping in the breeze.

"Fairy magic," Grumplestick grunted. "Keeps camp a secret."

At the entrance to camp, a large wooden sign read:

WELCOME TO CAMP MOONLIGHT

where being different is not unusual... it's *FUN*usual

Oliver snickered. "That's not even a real word—*fun*usual."

Norm grinned, doing his
best to *not* look like he
wanted to eat Oliver.
He didn't want to
eat anybody. But he
could go for a nice
bowl of berry casserole.

Norm's stomach growled so loudly that
Oliver jumped.

"Don't eat me!" said Oliver.

"Will you quit it?" Norm whispered.

Grumplestick went on and on, doing a
lot of pointing with his clipboard.

" . . . and that's the dining hall, with
the red, log roof," finished Grumplestick.

"Where they serve the best berry
casserole," said a voice from right
behind them.

Oliver shrieked and jumped closer to Norm.

A slender gray creature with a big, oval head and peanut-shaped pupils stood watching them. She had three very, very long fingers on each hand that were currently pressed together, impatiently tapping. She did not look amused.

"I am Zeena Morf, your counselor," she said. "I came from . . ."

"Outer space?!" said Oliver.

"No," Zeena said. "From my cabin. The one right next to yours."

Norm and Oliver followed Zeena's long, gray arm and long, gray finger. It pointed to one of several cabins with a 4 painted on the door.

Zeena opened the screen door and led Norm and Oliver inside.

"These are your campmates."

A brown rabbit with long antlers on her head raced around Norm and Oliver, stopping between her rapid questions to look them up and down or thump her foot.

"Hey there! Wow, you're big. Like really big. And furry. Lots of fur. So much fur. But not you. You're small. You don't have any fur. Why don't you have any fur? Did you shed your fur? Did you ever have fur?"

"This is Hazel," said Zeena. "She'll be staying in the cabin with the other girl campers."

"Hazel, that's me," she said. "I'm a jackalope. Ever heard of a jackalope? Part jack rabbit, part antelope. A jackalope!"

She leaned in close to Norm and Oliver and whispered, "I also might be part raccoon, on my mother's side."

"She eventually stops talking," said a boy with pointed ears poking out from under a mop of blue hair. He had wings on his back, and Norm couldn't help but notice that one was much smaller than the other.

"I'm Wisp. I took a bottom bunk. Is that cool? I kinda have trouble reaching high places."

He closed his eyes, squeezed his fists, and fluttered his wings. He managed to lift a couple of inches off the ground, but no higher. That little wing just couldn't do it.

"One of these days," he sighed.

"Hey, that was pretty good!" said Norm. "Your feet weren't touching the ground at all!"

"I have feet," said Hazel. "Two feet. Two big feet. But not as big as your feet. Big feet. Hey, are you a Bigfoot?"

Zeena sighed. "We will begin our first activity bright and early tomorrow morning."

"What will we be doing?" asked Norm.

"Canoe skills," Zeena said. "All first-time campers are taught basic canoe skills."

Norm's stomach dropped. How was he going to fit in a canoe? He wasn't even sure he would fit in the bunk bed!

"On the lake?" Oliver gulped.

"No," said Zeena. "On top of the trees."

"Oh, good," said Hazel. "Glad it's not the lake. I don't want to get my fur wet. Do you know how long it takes to dry? A long time. And my antlers are top-heavy. They might tip. I'll tip. I might tip the canoe right over and then *SPLASH!*"

"Of course, the lake," Zeena said, burying her face in her hands. "Why would you canoe on top of . . . never mind. You should all get some rest. We have a long day tomorrow, and the earlier we get started, the better."

"Why is it better?" asked Oliver.

"The less chance we have of disturbing the lake monster," said Zeena.

Norm's eyes opened wide. Oliver's jaw dropped. Wisp's wings fluttered. Hazel rapidly thumped her foot.

"Did she—" Norm said.

"Just say—" Wisp said.

"Lake—" said Hazel.

"MONSTER?" finished Oliver.

MEANWHILE...

"A lake monster, eh?" said Barnaby Snoop.

He was hiding behind a tree, close to Cabin 4, and listening to every word. He raised his left eyebrow and then his right, and then he chuckled.

"If it's a lake monster they expect, then it's a lake monster they'll get. I have just the plan."

Norm did *not* get a good night's sleep. When he put his head on the pillow, his feet stuck way out over the end of the bed. When he pulled his feet up, his head poked out over the other end of the bed. By the time he found a comfortable way to curl up, the sun was rising, and Zeena was at the door to their cabin.

"Rise and shine, campers," she said.
"Time for a good breakfast
and then . . . basic
canoe skills."

"Um, pardon me?" asked Oliver. "Did you . . . did you say something about a lake *monster*?" From the dark circles under his eyes, he looked like he got as much sleep as Norm did.

"Not to worry, that's just an old camp legend," said Zeena. "Maybe." She turned and headed toward the dining hall. "Follow me."

After breakfast, Zeena led them down to Shadow Lake, where Grumplestick stood waiting, clipboard in hand. Norm wondered what the other campers were up to. The dining hall had been filled with a wild collection of campers.

There was a boy with bat wings, a fish-girl, and even a pair of twins with horns and goat legs! But, like Norm had expected, he towered over all of them.

A low mist hung over Shadow Lake. Two canoes sat along the shore, half in the water and half on the sandy beach.

Norm scratched his head, wondering if the canoe would hold his weight.

Hazel nervously thumped her foot.

"I am not going in that water," said Oliver.

"Why not?" said Grumplestick.

"Because there's a monster in that lake!" said Wisp.

"You mean the ol' creature of Shadow Lake?" said Grumplestick.

Norm, Oliver, Wisp, and Hazel all nodded.

Grumplestick waved them off. "That's just an old camp legend. A tall tale."

They all let out a sigh of relief.

"Maybe," said Grumplestick. "Okay, on to canoeing. Norm and Oliver, you're partners. Wisp and Hazel, you're together. First step: life vests."

Zeena and Grumplestick helped the campers adjust the straps and tighten their vests. Oliver's was so big on his skinny body that he couldn't move his head left or right. Norm's was so small that it couldn't be fully strapped. Wisp had a vest small enough to fit a doll, with just enough room for his wings to stick out. Hazel's fit fine, but she kept buckling and unbuckling the clasps.

"Second step," said Grumplestick. "Get seated in the canoe. One in front, one in back."

Norm and Oliver eyed up the canoe like it was an alligator.

"I'll take the back," Norm said with a wheeze. His vest was too tight.

"Did you say something?" asked Oliver. He tried to turn to hear Norm better, but the vest was so puffy it covered his ears.

Norm pointed at Oliver and then at the front of the canoe.

Oliver gave Norm a big thumbs-up and climbed into the front of the canoe.

Norm put one foot in the canoe. The canoe sunk into the sand. He held the side and put his other foot in. The canoe sunk even lower. Norm had a bad feeling about this.

"Balance is everything," said Grumplestick, marching along the beach with his clipboard and whistle.

"Balance. Got it," said Norm. He carefully lined himself up with the middle of the back seat and sat down.

The second he did, the front end of the canoe shot up in the air and catapulted Oliver right out of it . . . and into Shadow Lake with a *SPLASH!*

Oliver thrashed and flailed his arms in the water. "Help! Help, I can't swim! It's got me! The monster's got me!"

"Oliver?" said Grumplestick.

"Yes?"

"Stand up," said Grumplestick.

Oliver stopped thrashing and flailing and stood up. The water came up to his knees, and the only thing grabbing him was a piece of lake weed wrapped around his ankle.

"I knew that," said Oliver. His cheeks were very red.

Grumplestick scribbled something on his clipboard.

After a few more tries, Norm and Oliver had the balance part down. Norm had to sit in the very middle of the canoe, *between* the seats and Oliver . . . well, it didn't matter where Oliver sat. So, he took a seat in the front of the canoe. Better to see the lake creature that way, if it decided to show up.

Hazel and Wisp had their own challenge: keeping Hazel in one seat. She was up, she was down. She was at the front of the canoe, she was at the back.

"If you don't sit down and stay in your seat," said Wisp, "I'm going to splash your fur with lake water!"

Hazel gasped. "You wouldn't!"

"I would if that's what it'll take to keep you from tipping this canoe over."

Hazel reluctantly took her seat.

Meanwhile, Norm and Oliver sat as still as possible. Their canoe sat so low in the lake that any sudden movement might fill it with water.

"Okay, campers," said Grumplestick. "The next step is rowing in a straight line." He pointed to an orange cone floating away from the beach. "You'll have to work together, coordinating your oar strokes,

so that you can paddle to the cone, turn, and come back to shore. Left, then right, then left, then right . . . easy as that."

Wisp and Hazel went first. Going in a straight line did not look as easy as Grumplestick made it sound. When Wisp paddled on the left, Hazel paddled three times on the right. When Wisp paddled three times on the left, Hazel paddled six times on the right.

"We're going in circles!" said Hazel. "Around and around and around in a circle. Why do you think that is, Wisp? Why do you think we're going in circles? Did you know we were going in circles? A circle is *not* a straight line, Wisp. It's not!"

"I know what a circle is!" cried Wisp. "You have to stop rowing so much each time!"

Hazel scratched her antlers and thumped her foot. "Huh. Who knew?"

Grumplestick scribbled on his clipboard some more.

"Norm and Oliver . . . now it's your turn."

Oliver turned to the side and gave Norm a thumbs-up. Norm gave Oliver a thumbs-up in return.

Oliver dipped his paddle into the water and pushed, with two hands and all of his might.

Norm dipped his paddle into the water and pushed, with one hand and just a little bit of his might.

The canoe veered off to one side.

"Switch sides," said Norm, trying to get them back on track.

But Oliver couldn't hear him. His life vest covered most of his head.

"Crisp fries? How should I know what they're serving for lunch, Norm? Right now, we need to figure out how to paddle and get this over with before the lake monster shows up!"

No sooner had Oliver said "lake monster" that Norm saw something. Something in the water.

"Oliver, look!" Norm said. He pointed his oar out toward the middle of the lake.

Oliver also stopped paddling. "Is that . . . ?"

"Th-the monster of Shadow Lake!" Norm finished.

A single eye on top of a long, thin stalk had slowly risen above the surface of the water . . . and it was looking right at them!

MEANWHILE...

"I spy, with my little eye . . . a Bigfoot!" said Barnaby Snoop.

Barnaby pressed his eye against the periscope of his one-person submarine.

"Once you are back out here in the middle of the lake tomorrow, I'll just motor under your canoe, reach up with my submarine's mechanical claw, and swoop you up in a net!"

He lowered the periscope and pedaled the submarine deeper.

"A genius plan, Snoop," he said to himself. "A most genius plan, indeed."

That night, Norm and Oliver told Wisp and Hazel all about what they had seen.

"And then," Norm said, "its one big eye poked out of the water, turned, and looked right at us."

"As soon as we saw it, it dipped back below the water," said Oliver.

"What are we going to do?" said Wisp.

"We'll tell someone," said Hazel. "That's what we'll do! We'll tell Zeena and Grumplestick. We'll tell the other campers. And the Army . . . and the Navy . . . and . . . "

"Hazel?" said Norm.

"Yes?"

"Deep breaths."

"Deep breaths, got it," she said.

When the camp owl hooted three times, it was time for lights-out. But none of them could fall asleep, not when they knew that tomorrow, they would have to face the monster of Shadow Lake.

"Okay, campers," said Grumplestick. "Today's the day."

Norm tried to keep his eyes open. Oliver snored while standing up. Hazel could hardly hold her antlers up, and Wisp's bloodshot eyes were hidden behind his mop of blue hair. None of them had slept a wink.

Grumplestick blared his whistle to wake them all up.

"I don't know what's gotten into you four, but if you think you can pass this canoe test in your sleep, you have another thing coming. Now put on your vests!"

Norm, Oliver, Hazel, and Wisp hustled for their vests while Grumplestick nodded and grumbled and scribbled things on his clipboard.

Norm wondered if Grumplestick was playing tic-tac-toe... against himself.

"In order to pass your canoe skills test, you will have to paddle out to Mystery Island, in the middle of the lake, and collect a flag to rescue Zeena."

"Wait," said Norm. "Our counselor is out on an island in the middle of the lake?"

"Yes," said Grumplestick. "She is stranded there. But she has s'mores. And you'll have s'mores, too, when you rescue her."

"Hello!" Zeena called, waving from the tiny island in the middle of the lake. "Can someone please get me off this island?"

"As you can see," said Grumplestick, "she needs your help . . . or at least sticks for making s'mores. Can't make s'mores without a good s'mores stick."

Oliver raised his hand. "But, um . . . Mr. Grumplestick, sir, there's a—"

"S'mores," said Grumplestick.

"In the lake," said Norm, "we saw—"

"S'mores," Grumplestick said.

Wisp said, "But—"

"S'mores."

Hazel thumped her foot. "If—"

"Wait, I know this one," said Norm. "S'mores."

"Hmmmm . . . " said Grumplestick, scribbling an X on his clipboard. "Ha, I won! Okay, glad we had that talk. Now let's get paddling."

MEANWHILE...

A lone periscope poked above the surface of the water. It swiveled toward Mystery Island. It swiveled back to shore. And then, ever so slowly, it dipped back below the surface of the water.

"Patience, Barnaby," he said. "A trap sprung in haste is a trap gone to waste!"

Barnaby Snoop knew that it was only a matter of time. He was going to get what he wanted. Barnaby Snoop *always* got what he wanted. And what he wanted, more than anything, was a Bigfoot.

But not just *any* Bigfoot. He wanted *this* Bigfoot. He wanted Norm.

orm and Oliver paddled across the middle of Shadow Lake toward Mystery Island. Toward Zeena Morf. And s'mores.

They followed Wisp and Hazel, who were following Grumplestick.

They paddled in a straight line without tipping over.

Dip, paddle, glide . . . dip, paddle, glide . . . dip, paddle, glide . . .

Suddenly, Norm heard a sound behind their canoe. The splash of something breaking the surface of the water. He turned, ever so slowly.

Staring at him, just out of arm's reach, was that eye stalk. That single, unblinking eye he and Oliver had seen yesterday in the middle of the lake.

"O-O-O-Oliver," Norm sputtered.

But Oliver couldn't hear him. Oliver couldn't hear anything with his life vest up around his ears.

"I think we're more than halfway there, Norm!" Oliver called over his shoulder.

"L-l-lake m-m-monster," Norm said.

The water rippled and bubbled, and Norm watched as the creature broke the surface of the water.

MEANWHILE...

"I've got you now!" Barnaby Snoop declared, pushing levers and pedaling to guide his one-man submarine out of the water.

The submarine bobbed on the surface of the lake, towering over the canoe. Cackling, Barnaby clapped his hands and pressed the big, red button labeled NET.

But nothing happened.

He pressed it again.

The motors whirred, the gears groaned. But still, nothing happened.

"Blasted machine!" cried Barnaby. He pressed the button harder.

The claw and net were caught on something . . . something below the water.

Barnaby pressed the button again. And again. He punched it with his fist. He slammed it with his elbow. He kicked it with his foot.

Still, nothing happened.

orm watched, horrified, as an orange, egg-shaped, metallic creature with a single eye stalk emerged from the water. It bobbed on the surface of the lake, casting a shadow over them.

"Must be some big clouds," Oliver called, over his shoulder, not looking back to see what Norm was seeing.

Norm tried to speak, but the words would not come out. So, he did the only thing he could think of. He put his long, awkward arms to use, reached out, and plucked Oliver right out of his seat at the front of the canoe and turned him around to see for himself.

"Norm?" Oliver squeaked. "That's . . . that's . . . "

"The lake monster!" Norm finished.

MEANWHILE...

No matter how many times Barnaby Snoop pressed that button, the claw and net would not work. They must be stuck.

"Blasted net!" cried Barnaby. He scrambled up the ladder, unscrewed the hatch, and popped his head out of the top of the submarine.

There was something under the water, under the submarine, something dark and big.

Norm and Oliver were frozen with fear. The monster was right behind them, making strange mechanical noises. And then, things got weirder.

"Look!" Oliver said. "The top of its head is opening up!"

Norm and Oliver watched as a strange, mustached man climbed out of the creature.

"Maybe it's a blowhole, like a whale?" said Norm. "That guy must have escaped!"

"Wait," said Oliver. "That's no creature. I think it's a boat!"

"A fishing boat!" said Norm. "And he's in trouble!"

"Don't worry, mister!" Oliver shouted. "We'll save you!"

"I'm going to throw you a life preserver!" Norm called.

Barnaby grinned. Could it really be this easy?

"Yes, yes, of course, I need to be saved!" Barnaby hollered back. "Save me! Oh, please save me!" Then he said, under his breath, "Once in your canoe, I'll just use my portable monster neutralizer. One zap and you'll be asleep for hours. And then it's just row, row,

row your boat back to shore. Barnaby always gets . . . *OOF!*"

The life preserver hit Barnaby Snoop so hard that it knocked him off the top of the submarine and into Shadow Lake with a *KERSPLASH!*

"Hold on, mister!" Oliver called. "We're coming!"

Norm and Oliver paddled their canoe around in a circle, aiming for the little mustached man holding onto the life preserver.

No matter how fast or how hard they paddled, they weren't going anywhere. It was like they were stuck in one spot.

"Oliver?" said Norm.

"Yes, Norm?" replied Oliver.

"Is it me, or are we going . . . *up*?" Norm said.

Oliver looked over the left side. Norm looked over the right. They were indeed rising into the air and out of the lake on the back of a giant, green, scaly creature.

A tail flipper bigger than their canoe broke the surface, spraying them

with water. A long neck rose up and turned toward Norm and Oliver. Two big, yellow eyes and a long snout filled with very sharp teeth swung toward them.

Norm and Oliver dropped their paddles and clutched each other in terror.

Then the creature sighed—a long, low, sad sigh—and looked back down toward the water.

Norm looked over the side. Oliver peeked over Norm's shoulder.

"She's stuck!" Norm said.

"It looks like a net!" said Oliver.

"I'll bet it's a fishing net," said Norm.

"From the fishing boat!" said Oliver. "That man must have been fishing and accidentally caught her in his net."

"Don't worry," Norm said, "we'll get you free."

The lake creature batted her big yellow eyes and purred.

No, no, no! Barnaby thought. It had all been going so well. *He* was supposed to be the lake creature! Not this *actual* lake creature. It was ruining everything! First, it showed up and got tangled in his net. Then, right when the Bigfoot and his friend were going to come pick him up in their canoe, they were sidetracked trying to untangle the creature! They were paying no attention to *him*!

"Help!" he cried. "I still need help! Save me! Forget about that creature! Save me FIRST! I'm a helpless man with absolutely no plans to capture you for my carnival! Wait . . . did I just say that last part out loud? Um . . . ha ha . . . pay no attention to that last part. I'll go ahead and save myself."

Wisp and Hazel paddled back as fast as they could. They could not believe their eyes—a real lake creature!

"Hi, Norm! Hi, Oliver! Hi, lake creature! I can't believe I'm meeting a real lake creature," said Hazel. "Do you live here all the time? Or are you on vacation? I like vacations. One time, I went to a lake for vacation. But not this lake. One that didn't have any lake creatures. I did meet a catfish named . . . "

"Hazel?"

"Yeah, Wisp?" Hazel said.

"Let's help untangle her from the net."

The lake creature lowered Norm and Oliver back into the water. With the net wrapped around her tail flipper, she couldn't swim back down to the bottom of the lake.

"This net definitely belongs to that orange fishing boat," said Oliver.

"That orange fishing boat must belong to the little mustached man," growled Norm. "He needs to be more careful where he fishes!"

Norm, Oliver, Hazel, and Wisp looked for the mustached man in the life preserver, but he was already gone. And so was the life preserver.

"Where'd he go?" asked Wisp.

"Oh look!" said Hazel. "There he is! On the beach. Wow, he sure is a fast swimmer. He's waving to us!" Hazel waved back. "No, no . . . he's shaking his fist at us. He's so excited that he's shaking his fist. That's nice. What a nice man."

The lake creature growled and glared back at the beach.

"Okay, Cabin 4," said Norm, "let's free our friend here."

Norm used his long arms to pull the net up as high as he could from her flipper while Oliver slipped his skinny arms in to untangle the net.

"Almost there!" Oliver said. "The end of the net is . . . just . . . out . . . of reach."

"I know!" said Wisp. He held his breath and flapped his wings as fast as he could.

Even though he couldn't fly, he created enough wind to push the end of the net toward Oliver.

"Got it!" said Oliver.

Hazel worked her antlers under the tangled netting. "Just a little higher, Norm."

"Not a problem!" Norm said. He stood as tall as he could and lifted his arms over his head.

It was enough space for Hazel to cut through the netting with her front teeth.

And just like that, the creature was free!

She batted her eyes and purred and smiled with her long row of sharp, jagged teeth.

Norm, Oliver, Wisp, and Hazel watched as she flipped on her back and blew a long geyser of water up into the air.

"I guess that means *thank you?*" said Wisp.

She swam a circle around them, slapped the water with her tail, and then disappeared below the surface of Shadow Lake.

"Huh, so there *was* a lake creature after all," Norm said.

"A friendly lake creature, at that," Oliver added.

"Guys look! Look guys!" said Hazel. "That guy's fishing boat is sinking. It's sinking! Can we save it? Should we save it?"

"Too late," said Wisp.

The orange submarine rolled over onto its side and ever so slowly, sunk down under the surface of the lake.

Norm and Oliver groaned.

"How's he going to fish now?" asked Norm.

"Oh man," said Oliver. "He seemed like such a nice man, too."

"Guess we'd better get these s'mores sticks to Mystery Island," said Norm.

"Yeah," said Oliver, "and get our canoe skills certification!"

By the time the campers pulled their canoes onto the shore, Zeena and Grumplestick had a nice campfire going on Mystery Island.

"What took so long?" asked Zeena. "I almost started making these s'mores without you."

"I wondered if you had given up," said Grumplestick.

"There was a lake creature!" said Oliver.

"And she was stuck in a net," added Norm.

"A lake creature?" said Grumplestick.

"In a net?" said Zeena.

"The net belonged to a fishing boat," said Wisp.

"And the fishing boat belonged to a nice, little mustached man," added Hazel.

"A fishing boat?" said Grumplestick.

"Belonging to a nice, little mustached man?" Zeena said.

Norm, Oliver, Hazel, and Wisp all nodded.

"Well, that's unusual," said Grumplestick.

Norm smiled. "Don't you mean *fun*usual?"

Grumplestick scribbled something on his clipboard.

There was a long pause.

A long, awkward pause.

"I have one thing to say to you campers." Grumplestick turned the clipboard to show the others. Attached to it was an evaluation sheet filled with checkmarks and smiley faces. And a game of tic-tac-toe. "Congratulations on earning your canoe skills certification!"

"Now, who wants s'mores?" said Zeena.

A geyser of water sprayed up in the middle of Shadow Lake, where a dark shape appeared for only a moment.

MEANWHILE...

Beyond Mystery Island, at the farthest
end of Camp Moonlight, a soggy, lake-
weed-covered Barnaby Snoop wriggled free
of his life preserver and wrung the water
out of his mustache.

"You may have won this round, you creature campers, but mark my words . . . Barnaby Snoop *always* gets what he wants!"

He dumped out a boot full of water and lake gunk. "And right now, Barnaby Snoop wants some dry clothes."

THE END?

ABOUT THE AUTHOR

Joe McGee teaches creative writing at Sierra Nevada College. An avid cartoonist, board game player, and role-playing gamer, Joe is also the author of the *Junior Monster Scouts* chapter book series and three picture books: *Peanut Butter & Brains*, *Peanut Butter & Aliens*, and *Peanut Butter & Santa Claus*. He lives in a quiet little river town with his wife (also a children's book author) and their puppy, Pepper.

ABOUT THE ILLUSTRATOR

Bea Tormo is a children's book illustrator by day and a comic artist by night. She lives near Barcelona, Spain, where she enjoys being part of a community of artists. Besides children's books, Bea works on comic books, magazines, webcomics, and fanzines. She especially loves drawing grumpy people and monsters.